Sex lover: Jovita's sex story

By Susan R. Garza

Table of content

Chapter 1

100 days before the wedding

"What's up, Jovita? There, you seem to be quite confused." Following my registration, Adam stated.

"Yeah. Sorry." My long, black hair flew everywhere as I remarked while shaking my head.

As he grinned his huge goofy smile at me, Adam's blue eyes began to pierce my light brown ones. He was adorable. I couldn't see myself having a sexual relationship with him. More of the best buddy.

Why do you ask? As I turned to look at a handsome guy, a deep voice flooded my ears.

With unruly black hair and dark eyes, he stood roughly 6'3". I could immediately see myself on top of him since his physique was athletically fit.

I said, "Sorry, what?

"I must load this cash into my prepaid card." I was given a wad of ones while he spoke.

I rolled my eyes as Adam began to giggle to my left, and I began to count.

Then I said, "One."

This guy was trapping me against a wall in my mind. My nails rubbed down his back as he bit my neck. He would raise me by holding onto my legs. I enclose him in my legs.

"One hundred eighty-eight." I exhaled heavily as I completed.

"All OK, add it all." He commanded.

I wanted to say something sarcastic to catch his eye, but if I wanted to leave my job, it wasn't going to be over some random man.

I loaded the whole amount of cash into his card and then I let the receipt print. I looked up at him as I handed him the slip and felt his palm on mine. As I yanked my hand away, he was grinning at me.

Enjoy your day, please. With clenched teeth, I said.

I was relieved to see him depart as he walked away joyfully. I was unable to allow myself to become very enthused about a man.

Kelvin Wood, I believe. The largest man whore in town, according to Adam,

The catch, therefore, is what? I inquired.

He doesn't have sex, "He does everything but doesn't have sex for some reason," he said with a smirk as I furrowed my eyes.

That is very tacky. Not worth my time, I scowled.

After leaving work, I hurried to my sister's place to sample some cakes. The cake was my favorite food, but I detested the fact that my sister had chosen to wed the worst jerk on the planet.

What about this one? After I had had my sixth cake, she questioned.

"It's just cake," I informed her.

"It's not just cake. What if the one I choose is too elegant? Or was it acting too briskly?" I raised my fork to her as she began to scream.

"It's just cake," "Shit, I'm going to be late," I said as I sat down and glanced at my phone.

As I laced up my boots, I put my plate down. I staggered out her back door and saw my sister waving at me.

I ran to group therapy right away. The head hancho, a black lady, sat on the other side of me in a room that was set up with chairs arranged in a circle. Her area of specialization as a psychologist was an addiction.

Let's welcome Jovita Joel to the class as our newest member. I jumped as she made a gesture my way and whispered "hello."

The black lady gave Kelvin a stern nod for being late as he moved past me and sat down next to me. Since I had just returned to the area, it was my first time participating in this group, so I was surprised to see him.

Therefore, Jovita, share with us a fantasy you've had since moving to the area. Everyone was looking at me when she said this.

Well, this one man entered the shop today and passed through my queue. I started "and handed me $138 in one-dollar bills. I also saw myself being pushed into a wall by him, and I wanted it. So terrible."

I hurried out of class as soon as possible to avoid Kelvin talking to me, but when I attempted to unlock my vehicle door, he stopped me.

I guess you're daydreaming about me. He gave a wink.

I want to go home. I erupted.

Tell me which portion you liked most. "Me biting your neck or grasping your ass?" he smirked as he whimpered.

I wailed on his chest as he seized hold of my ass with a tight grip while grinning. He gave my ass a little smack before releasing his hold while chuckling wickedly.

"I-" He cut me off as I was beginning.

Would you want to leave this place? He gave a wink.

Chapter 2

95 days before the wedding.

Get the heck out of here. As Kelvin stood up and put on his boxers, I sighed in pain.

What is your issue? "Most ladies are cool with it," he yelled furiously.

I'm not, however. "If you're going to fuck with me, you're going to push your penis inside of me," I replied.

He laughed, "Make me.

"Don't tempt me." I lost it "I can't pretend to be OK with your silly little rule like other females can. Simply carry it out."

"I can't." In my face, he hissed.

Then we're through here. You were just nude, I chuckled as I put on my clothing.

And you're fortunate that I went that far, He disputed.

"Jovita!" I could hear my sister speaking. I turned to see Kelvin enter my room, still only partially clothed.

Don't fucking move, I say. I yelled as I hurried outside to the living room and watched my sister enter the home with a stack of papers.

Hey, I need your assistance with a seating plan. She asked, "Wait who-" as she placed everything on the table.

"All right, I can assist, but I'm amid someone.." I muttered.

What brand of shirt do you have on? I questioned as I cast my gaze downward at the white men's t-shirt.

"Mine." As Kelvin exited the building shirtless and smirked at my sister, his rich voice sent shivers down my spine "keep my shirt. Later, I'll return to get it."

"Or I'll give it to you in group," she said. I said.

"You don't want me to come back? Owch." He laughed.

Not after what just occurred, I say. I yelled, not realizing my sister was present.

"I'd better go," you said. "See you soon," Kelvin said while turning to face Sara and grinning at me.

Whatever, I muttered.

He grinned at Sara and walked out of the home. As Sara furrowed her brows at me, I groaned and ran my fingers through my hair.

'Kelvin Wood' You know he doesn't, she inquired.

Yes, I came to that conclusion. Okay, the seating configuration, I snarled.

After setting her papers down on the table, Sara went back to her papers. My role was to monitor and be watchful as she began to allocate individuals to locations.

You cannot place Alyssa near Tyler without risking a "you dumped me" breakdown, I beg you. As she made the necessary corrections, I called attention to them.

"Next is Payson and Kyle. Really?" After an hour or so, we had completed everything after she repaired it as well.

"I must go to work. Adam's night duty." I grinned as I removed Kelvin's shirt from me.

—

He just refused to carry it out, As I laughed with Adam, he laughed as well.

"He wouldn't, and I have no idea why. And I was irritated by it." So I was about to throw him out when my sister stepped in, and I complained.

What was her response? He giggled.

She was as shocked by my giving him a chance as you are, she said. I grinned and said, "I wish he would just do it."

Two blond ladies entered the room, setting some drinks on the belt in front of me while wearing a little too much makeup and acting a little too excitedly.

Do you have your ID with you? I inquired.

I find it hard to believe you connected us with kelvin. stated one.

He abides by this guideline. The less beautiful blond was cautioned.

"I d's?" As Kelvin approached them and grinned at my outrage, I questioned.

I wasn't expecting him to be that seductive. Less beautiful one muttered.

Give me your stupid IDs, or go out, I say. They glanced at me, and I snapped.

As Kelvin gave Adam his whole attention, Adam was giggling beside me. Before he signaled to the females to hand over their IDs, I heard a low growl.

They were joyfully removed from my hair when I checked for alcohol. Preppy, giggly blond types drove me crazy.

"We'll see you tomorrow at the group." Before departing, he grinned.

Think you could convince him to stop quicker than two blondes?" I turned to face Adam and he asked.

Is it a difficult task? I smirked "You can count on me. For Jovita Joel, Kelvin Wood is not a challenge."

Chapter 3

87 days before the wedding.

Do you believe it's a good idea to play with another male? Does it hinder your ability to recover? I was sitting with my arms crossed over my chest when the lady inquired.

"Ms. Poole, I like sex." And to be truthful, who I have sex with and who I don't have sex with is nobody's business, I said. I shouldn't even be a part of this ridiculous crew.

However, you are present for a purpose. She recalled me, which made me shudder.

Kelvin turned to face me with a worried expression as tears threatened to spill from my eyes. I stood up and walked over to the entrance after grabbing my sweatshirt.

"You and I are different in that I don't pressure them to be perfect," I said. I said, "I don't act as if there's nothing wrong with me. I recognize that I am not flawless. You are so defective that you believe you can instruct us on how to behave and whom to fuck, for example.

"That isn't accurate." She debated.

"None of us are bothered by your lectures. We all continue to want sex. "Isn't that correct, kelvin?" I yelled.

I gave a little wink and walked out of the room to go home. I didn't need any of this nonsense. She has no right to mention that I was there for a purpose. I'm not to blame for my sex addiction.

Sara texted, "So what time are you picking me up?"

*Roughly 11:00. Check to see whether the other females are prepared to go out tonight. I responded and put my phone on the table.

When I opened my door in response to a knock, kelvin was standing there, furiously staring down at me. Before shoving me inside and closing the door behind him, he grinned.

I said, "W-what are you doing?"

"Be quiet." Before pushing me up against a wall, he snapped.

He tightened his grip on my waist and pressed his lips onto mine. My body lied to me and returned the kiss, tangling my fingers in his hair, and pulling just a little. He grabbed my ass and squeezed it while groaning into my lips.

"I want to work something out with you." Against my lips, he roared.

"Okay?" I remarked as I gave him another kiss.

As long as you keep giving me sex, we can have it, he said after pausing to collect his breath.

"You mean to fucking be your toy?" I lost it.

Yes, kind of. He shrugged.

"Okay." He gave me a gentle kiss and released me as I giggled.

But until I tell you to stop, you have to keep delivering it to me. I don't cope well with rejection, he said.

"Okay. purely sexual only. "No relationship nonsense," I said.

"Deal." He murmured before scooping me up and encircling me by my legs.

He tightened his grip on my thighs as our lips made contact. As he lay me on the sofa on top of him, I groaned against his lips.

"Wait." I said, "I Uhm, I have plans tonight," as he bit my neck.

"And a different guy?" He roared indignantly.

Girls' night, please. As he stood up, I chuckled and said, "With my sister and several females."

"All right, I'll go along." He chose.

On a ladies' night? You're aware that entails rating males while drinking in a pub, right? I queried.

I'll wait here till you return, so please do. He declared.

"I suppose." You may stay here if you want to crash, but no snuggling, I shrugged. Since we are completely sexual, you know.

He grinned while nodding his head. He ripped off his shirt and threw it at me quicker than I could react. I undid my shirt and put on his saggy one instead.

"You like putting on my clothing." He grinned.

"I prefer loose-fitting clothing, and you're obese," I punned.

"You refer to yourself as a fat chaser?" He gave me a raised eyebrow.

"Perhaps I am," I said as I entered the bathroom and began to curl my hair.

Why are you still single, then? From the living room, he screamed.

I guess you could say I'm damaged. I chuckled as a lovely curl tumbled down my back.

"Me too." "Are you the sort of lady who wants to be married and have kids one day?" he joked as he watched me enter the restroom.

"I'm not sure," "I can't find a guy who understands my requirements," I shrugged.

How many men/women have you shared a bed with? He queried.

"What's up with all these inquiries?" I lost it.

Wow, that's a high number, huh? As I finished doing my hair, he winked.

It shouldn't matter, however. Please refrain from making assumptions about people's pasts. a fresh start with us Deal?" I lost it.

"Deal." I've been with 13," he said with a grin.

"Six." I said, "Nearly seven." I grinned.

"Six? Really? Just six? He questioned with a perplexed expression.

I said, "Six. I once dated a sex addict. He occupied the majority of my attention for about two years, on and off. The other men were simply, you know, casual lovers or serious flings. Nothing unusual

He strolled closely behind me as I made my way to my bedroom. He sat on my bed while I searched for a dress while just wearing a bra and underwear.

Red seems to be your hue, I think." As I got my red dress and put it on, he grinned.

It was the perfect length and wasn't either too long or too short. Kelvin grinned at me before taking a big swallow. I grabbed my phone and turned to face him since I thought I looked nice.

Don't do anything unclean on my bed, please. I said, "My fridge is stocked with food. I'll be back in a couple of hours, so feel free to eat.

—-

"A seven." The guy in a suit at the far end of the bar was made fun of by Sara.

"Nine." "I admire a guy who knows how to dress," I grinned.

Is he up for it? Kelly pointed to a tall, black guy and inquired.

I like eating black meat. At my left, Heather purred.

"Four." I gave a head nod.

Four? questioned Heather.

"He has that gangster appearance, and I'm not like thugs," she said. I sighed.

How do you know he is a criminal? She asked.

Baggy clothing and trousers that extend beyond his ass. I said the obvious: "He wants to be a thug or a thug. He must call his female partners mama.

"Go investigate for me."

Heather guffawed.

What benefit do I get from this? I lost it.

I'll pay for another attempt. She grinned.

I pondered it and then said, "Okay."

I stood up from my chair and approached the guy who was gathered with some of his pals. I sat next to him, and he seemed happy with how I looked.

I'm Jovita. Hello. He returned my grin, and so did I.

"Reese here.

"Well, Reese, my buddy kind of has a crush on you. Before she approaches you, I wanted to ask you a few things because of the way you appear. I queried.

"Of sure, mama, ask away."

First strike, mommy.

I questioned, "Do you have a job?"

Mommy, I'm just standing up for my team, that's all for now. He grinned.

Crew, strike two.

Do you have children, too? I queried.

Oh, baby mother conflict. Did Haley send you to speak with me here? He exploded.

Three strikes. baby mother

You're done.

That's all, thanks. "Nope."

Where's my shot? I moved back over to the females and yelled while raising my hands.

"Wannabe gangster or real?" She questioned as she passed me a shot, which I eagerly downed.

"Wanna be" is my best guess. But I could be mistaken. Anyway, I have someone waiting for me at home, I shrugged. So I had best go on.

"Is that tasty gentleman from yesterday there?" Sara flubbed.

"kelvin?" Kelly enquired in shock.

I agree, kelvin. "I cracked the code," I rolled my eyes.

I stood up and stumbled over for a second before regaining my strength and looking at Sara.

"I love you sister but I have to go." I laughed, "I'll talk to you soon."

Chapter 4

82 days before the wedding

Why don't you simply finish it already? I sat bare on top of kelvin and hissed.

I've simply not had any sex in a long. As I massaged his member against me and moaned in his ear, he paused.

Give me some time, Jovita. As I inserted the tip, he moaned.

As I moved a bit closer, his eyes rolled to the back of his head. He recklessly bit his bottom lip and grasped my ass.

You like that, right? I spoke softly in his ear.

You're so close. He swiftly raised his hips while exhaling to get most of himself inside of me.

'Ow' is used. He grinned like it was a joy to his ears as I complained.

As soon as I began to ride him, he pushed up even more. I moved my body up and down on top of him because he felt so fantastic inside of me. He was larger and meaner than I had anticipated.

He grabbed my hips and smacked me behind to get me to go over to him. After some time, he had me go down on all fours and was grabbing me from behind. firmly grabbing and yanking my hair.

I could see he hadn't had sex in a long, and by pushing this intercourse on him, I was probably only aggravating his addiction.

"Uhh." As I unleashed on him, he moaned.

As he entered me, I could feel the pulse of his member. He sat down next to me while he attempted to regain his breath, and I leaned back and relaxed.

If you want to spend the night, I will be back late since I have to, well, go meet my sister tonight.

"I suppose I could remain." He exhaled before putting on his boxers "Those were good. I'm grateful."

"Oh gosh." As I stood up and put on my clothes, I moaned "Do not thank me for the sex. Are we already 15?"

He hissed, "No.

"Okay, don't say thank you," I chuckled and said, "I'll come back later," as I brushed my hair and applied makeup in front of the mirror.

My sister had a really exciting night in store for us. She decided to have a Halloween party as a type of self-empowerment celebration.

"Bob for the Apple, darts, and locate the candy corn," said the speaker. As I rocked the infant back and forth, she clapped her hands collectively.

Tinley certainly snoozes a lot. I snorted at the infant who was dozing off in my arms.

She is a newborn. Sara made a mention.

"Clearly." I grinned and rolled my eyes "So, how is Kye doing? He is not someone I often see."

He is spending the evening with the guys. He seems to not want to spend any time with me lately, she complained.

"Shivering jitters." I sighed.

Jitters? she questioned.

He is anxious about getting hitched. I answered, "It is quite typical. You've never watched a romantic comedy, have you?"

Naturally, I have. She chuckled.

"Would it be okay if I brought a guest to your Halloween party? maybe a few people?" I questioned as I put Tinley to sleep.

Oh, Kelvin, did you mean that? She chuckled.

Indeed, kelvin. I grinned and said, "I want to see if I can get him out with me in public."

"Do you feel vulnerable lately? That he won't accompany you out of the bedroom?" She made up a gasp.

"Not uneasy." I said, "Just wondering,"

She questioned, "Curious?"

Relationships aren't my thing, but he may as well be my arm candy at your wedding if he's going to be around. I sighed.

You intend to invite Kelvin to my wedding, right? It's sort of a couple of things, she enquired.

"By then, we'll essentially be dating," I said.

"I'll let you skip your speech at the wedding if you can convince him to show up to the Halloween party." She grinned.

Is this a wager? I chuckled.

"Sort of. I'm curious too." She grinned.

"Deal."

Chapter 5

Until The Wedding, 73 Days

What is it like for you to live alone? I grinned at Adam, who had recently moved into his apartment after leaving his girlfriend's home.

There is no joy today. I'm too sad about Carly, he moaned.

What happened? He bagged it at the end of my register after I inquired while I scanned the things.

"She became involved with kelvin." Not hooked up because you know him, but she toyed with him numerous times, and when he rejected her a few days ago, she was enraged enough to tell me, he grumbled as he hoisted a bag into a cart.

"I apologize." "I know how Kelvin is," I groaned.

"So do I." He shrugged.

Okay, I've got a thought. I grinned.

Why is it there? He queried.

"Tonight is my sister's Halloween party. Why don't you follow us?" As a faint smile appeared on his face, I grinned.

Do I have to wear a costume? I chuckled, and he grinned.

If you don't want to, then no. "I'm going to be a bunny," I grinned.

A seductive bunny I bowed my head as he gave a wink.

I'll see you tonight, then. He excitedly nodded and I said, "Good."

-

I put on my fishnet stockings and gave myself one final look in the mirror. I was wearing a black frock with black rabbit ears and a little black cotton tail that didn't quite reach my butt.

"God. Do you need to dress that way?" Kelvin adjusted his tie while groaning behind me.

It's the first and probably final time I'll ever see him dressed in a suit. He seemed fantastic. He was going as an entrepreneur. He refers to it as a con artist.

"I assume you like my costume," He smacked my ass, and I giggled.

"Do I need to leave? Don't you think that will give the impression that we are a couple?" He queried.

"No." I said, shaking my head, "I invited Adam, too."

"Adam? That young thug from the shop?" He gripped my waist and yanked me back into his chest as he snarled down my back.

"That's right, punk," He's my FRIEND, I said.

"Okay, ok." With his hands up in the air, he added, "Maybe I'll stay home."

Home? I questioned.

Oh, I've been here for days; I pretty much live here. When did you start hanging out with Adam outside of work, he questioned.

Since you had a sexual encounter with his ex-girlfriend, he is upset since she was dumped. I declared.

"Well, what?" It's not your responsibility to be his shoulder to weep on, he said, almost seeming delighted that he had ruined Adam and his relationship.

It kind of is since he is his buddy. As I slid his sweatshirt over my shoulders, I chuckled.

"No, it's not at all," His arms were crossed over his chest as he spoke.

'Are you envious?' He spread his arms out and snarled at me as I grinned.

I'm not envious. He declared.

It was a calm trip to the party. I accused kelvin of being envious, and he immediately appeared to want nothing to do with me. He seemed to be envious.

"Hello, come on in!" As we entered, my sister waved for us and grinned at me.

The wager was successful.

I won't be speaking at their wedding.

God is good.

Let's have a drink now, I say. Kelvin followed me into the kitchen as I gestured for him to do so.

Where is lover boy, then? He grinned.

"Just being late, Adam. He is coming." I responded by grinning back.

My head started to feel dizzy after 10 shots. After 10 shots, Kelvin was still as sober as a rock and seemed unimpaired. He was twice my size, however. I suppose that explains it.

"Adam!" When Adam arrived and excitedly hugged me, I grinned.

Hey, thanks for the invitation. As I gave him another embrace, he grinned.

"No issue. I found kelvin to be uninteresting regardless. Thank you for coming." Kelvin hissed at me from behind as I laughed.

It's not like you to invite me anywhere, I mean. He mock-punched me in the arm and chuckled.

We have a friendship. "You're down, I'm down," I grinned.

When Kelvin squeezed my butt forcefully and laughed behind me, our prolonged eye contact ended.

I'll go look for something to do. Before exiting the room, he stated.

Do you want a drink, then? I questioned while I was perched on the counter.

Sure, he responded.

I felt wonderful after five more shots. I had the impression that anything was within my power to do. Instead of wearing his uniform, Adam looked wonderful, and a part of me was drawn to him.

"So it seems like you two are tight." He remarked.

Yes, when he's not being a jerk. I chuckled and said, "You know, I need someone a bit less snarky."

I drew nearer to Adam and wrapped one arm over his neck while holding a red Solo cup in the other.

"Me?" At me, he furrowed his brows.

"Okay!" It's time for us to go right now, Kelvin almost screamed.

He pulled me away from Adam, who seemed to be amused by me, by grabbing me by the arm.

Kelvin dragged me home and threw me on the floor. I resisted going to bed. I yearned to go out and have a good time.

"Lay with me, baby." He undid his shirt and sat down to my left while I complained.

"Don't touch." As I massaged his arm, he exploded.

He watched as I climbed over and perched on top of him, bouncing on his crotch. Before shoving me off of him, he let out a loud moan.

"Avoid touching me. I'm not that person, and you're intoxicated." He exploded.

"Fine! Do not screw me. In any case, you don't even like me." I shouted, "I'm the girl who got you to have sex, therefore all I am to you is an easy fuck."

"Be quiet." He exploded.

And remember that, too! I screamed, "Keep in mind that I persuaded you to engage in sexual activity. I have what it takes, but none of these other gals did. The next time you reject me, you'd best keep it in mind!"

Chapter 6

The wedding is in 65 days.

kelvin said, "Fuck me like you mean it." As he grabbed me from behind, I groaned.

He rode me even harder after giving me a nasty ass slap. As he gasped in delight, my body stiffened and relaxed all over him.

Where did it go? He gave a deep laugh before thrusting into my weak area once again, which made me groan, and said, "That's right, moan for me...bitch."

He continued to slam me until I was gasping for breath and was unable to even groan. He then grabbed my hair, and I let out once more as he let out inside of me.

He pulled out and sat down next to me, and I could feel his pulse. I was taking a breath while he was doing the same.

Do you ever return home, then? I laughed as I put on my bra and pants.

"I prefer not to." He threw his shirt at me and shrugged while putting on his boxers and pants.

"Why?" I questioned as I dressed him and entered the kitchen.

"Excessive commotion." He grumbled, "Here, I like it. I have you here, and it's calm."

What romance! I made a joke while I was checking the cupboards.

Remember, we consumed the last box of food here. He grabbed his keys while grinning.

Where are you headed? I almost cried.

ALMOST.

"To visit the store In this home, food must be obtained." You work at a shop, how can you not have food in this home, he whined once again.

I dislike shopping, so I lost it.

"All right, let's get going. Put some trousers on." He spoke.

You put on a shirt. I lost it.

You possess my clothing. As I returned to the bedroom and put on a pair of leggings, he remarked.

"You own additional shirts. I like this." He gazed at me as I curled up in his white t-shirt.

"You may wear it now. Nevertheless, just because you look nice in it." He said as he pulled a scarlet shirt over his powerful frame.

Because it was late at night and only customers searching for ice cream and booze go shopping at that time, the store was empty.

"How about that? We like spaghetti." I rolled my eyes as he inquired while holding out a package of spaghetti.

Yes, it sounds wonderful. I shrug again.

"Let's say pizza. We eat pizza often." While examining several sorts, he laughed.

Pizza sounds tasty, all right. I sigh.

"God, you act like a little kid." He moaned as he piled pizza and spaghetti onto the trolley.

"Pizza and spaghetti cannot sustain us." Come on, let's walk to the produce section and peruse the fruit and veggies, I remarked.

"Let's go, I adore apples." He laughed.

As Kelvin strolled over to look at some apples, I saw the blond females from the previous day sorting through some apples. I remained by his side as we browsed the apples.

"kelvin! What's up?" One who had an orange face questioned.

"April, Heather." He grinned.

"Hannah." She was right.

Hannah, I'm sorry. She turned to look at me, and I gripped Kelvin's arm as he grinned.

I'm sorry, my name is Jovita. After pausing, he said, "Friend."

"Friend?" I tightened my grip on his arm as April giggled.

Like my best buddy, he shrugged.

"How did you do that? I've been trying for a long to be his...best buddy." Hannah gave me a grin.

Perhaps because I don't have an orange face from overuse of cosmetics. I grinned.

"Jovita." Kelvin reprimanded me.

"Pardon me?" She replied sharply.

"Excuse me—did I stutter?" As she turned to face her buddy in bewilderment, I grinned even more.

"Let's leave." Kelvin took hold of my arm and dragged me toward the checkout area.

"Kelvin, let go," I said. I grumbled.

What gives you the right to behave that way? As Dawn began to inspect our stuff for us, he snapped.

"Jovita, what are you doing here on your day off?" As he put our items in bags, Adam grinned.

purchasing items for the home. I grinned.

Also, Kelvin He feigned a wink.

He "kind of stays with me." I rolled my eyes and complained.

"Let's leave." As I bid goodbye to Adam and as we were leaving, Kelvin requested.

"Pizzas are almost done!" I entered the living room and sat down when Kelvin called from across the house.

"Hey! Would you want to see a movie?" I screamed back.

"Sure!" He screamed.

Without looking, I picked a movie and put it in. Kelvin gave me some pizza and sat down next to me as Fast & the Furious began playing on the TV.

Although I don't recall sleeping, I do remember Kelvin dragging me to the bedroom and tucking me in.

And we...

Cuddled...

Chapter 7

The wedding is in 54 days.

Hey, mind stopping by the bottle room on your break? Since that was the only area of the shop without cameras, Adam enquired.

I quickly entered the bottle room, making sure no one was looking. Adam was waiting for me next to the bottle dispenser. He gripped my waist and forced his lips on mine as I approached, grinning.

I hastily withdrew and cleaned my lips. I'm shocked by what he did. I took a step back and observed him.

What did it mean? I lost it.

You don't need Kelvin, I've been thinking ever since that party. He spoke.

That implies I need you, then. I lost it.

I can treat you better than kelvin, however, so no. He clarified.

I don't think so. I grinned.

"Don't you ever wonder what being in a true relationship might be like?" I leaned against the bottle filler as he requested.

It doesn't suit me, Adam, I suppose. I said, "With me, no true relationship ever works. I am an explosive time bomb."

"Jovita, you're my best buddy." And I believe we'd be fantastic together if you gave us a chance, he continued.

"Adam, I'm not sure." I moaned.

"Come over, look. You are welcome to visit on the day that we arrange. We can hang around and monitor the situation." He clarified.

"Okay." I chuckled and slapped him on the arm "Let's resume our work now. No more sentimental nonsense."

-

"kelvin!" When I entered the room and found him dozing off on the sofa, I shouted.

I took a sip of my vitamin water and then climbed up on top of him. He moaned and then looked at me as he made an effort to feel comfortable once again.

kelvin, aren't we kind of BFFs? I chuckled as I texted.

"Yeah." He motioned me aside.

So explain the cause to me. I grinned.

He questioned, "The reason?"

"The cause of your lack of sex." I was stuck.

"No," he yelled.

Please, kelvin. You never tell me anything about you, and you've met my sister, I cried, pouting.

He said, "I have a daughter."

You do, I questioned.

"I do." She is about a year old, he said with assurance.

"What is she called?" I queried.

Brea, he retorted.

"And where is she?" I queried.

"the mother. I now have visiting rights since they just relocated." He responded.

I questioned, "Do you want custody?"

"I do, of course. That's my child." He answered.

So Brea is the cause of your lack of sex, I take it? I queried.

"First, the addiction. After that, I just stopped having sex since I didn't want another Brea any time soon." He nodded, Not that you have in any way assisted my addiction.

Okay, pretend that I'm solely to blame. He grinned up at me as I laughed.

"As long as we're in this situation." He spoke of.

"No, our group will meet shortly. We must stop being late." I chuckled.

"Let's go on." He smirked "Rebel girl, get going. With me, skip."

He grabbed my hair and moaned, 'kiss me.'

Chapter 8

The wedding is in 40 days.

"Adam, ahh," He astonished me with how excellent he was in bed, and my gosh, was he fantastic.

"Yeah?" Both he and I moaned as I let go.

I backed away and put my underwear on before turning to face him. I couldn't believe I had slept with him, and I also felt bad about it. As if I were sleeping with kelvin.

"I should leave," He scowled at me as I giggled a bit.

"So I simply hit and quit?" you ask. At me, Adam hissed.

Kelvin is simply waiting for me, so that's all. I said softly.

After taking me out to lunch and to see a movie, Adam brought me back to his place for some lovely sex. Even just thinking about it gave me a headache.

Kelvin was waiting for me on the sofa when I hurried home. Although I wasn't in the mood for sex right now, I wouldn't say no if he came on.

"Your sister came over." "Something about the rehearsal dinner," he added.

That's in a few weeks, screw that. I sighed and said, "I can't wait for this wedding to be finished.

How was Adam's home doing? He sighed and got to his feet.

He flung his hands in the air, and I sighed, "Fine."

Do you consider me to be foolish, Jovita? "You had sex with him," he shouted.

"You virtually fuck with every female in town," So don't get in my face when I do it one god damn time, I shouted back.

Do you like playing the slut? He laughed.

I proceeded to shout back at him despite my injured sentiments, "Sorry, but WHO is a slut? Who Fucks someone who introduces themselves? Who?"

"Overcoming yourself now." And don't expect me to touch you tonight, he snarled.

Couldn't be more pleased I responded with a shout and shut the bathroom door behind me.

Why was Kelvin being so dreadfully envious? Not that we were dating or anything. He did not influence whatever I did. Both my father and my boyfriend are not him.

That much is true. He was adamant about not wanting a relationship with me.

God, you're so obstinate! Before the garage door slammed shut, I heard Kelvin shout.

Even though there wasn't anything wrong with his vehicle, he would go into the garage whenever we got into a dispute to work on it.

I suppose that was his attempt to de-stress.

As Kelvin cooked some spaghetti on the stove, I showered and got dressed in the towel.

It happened by mistake. I muttered.

An incident? Kelvin shoved me back against the counter after turning to face me.

I screamed back, "Yeah!

"just how? Has he just landed in your genitalia?" I tightened my hold on my towel as he roared.

No, but-" I sputtered.

"No. You fucked someone else because you weren't satisfied with what we had. Do you need me to make you forget about him for good?" He yelled.

"Yes," I muttered.

I was pushed into him when he grabbed me by the towel. As he pushed his lips into mine and kissed me, he had a menacing glare in his eyes.

Okay, I'll do that. He sighed.

Chapter 9

The wedding is in 20 days.

"Yet another month! Less than a month." I chewed on a pickle on the sofa while Sara walked back and forth.

Fearful? I made a note.

Just a little itch of the chilly feet, she said. She chuckled and took a seat next to me.

So how are things now? I questioned.

How is Kelvin doing these days? She grinned before giving me a wink.

I'm going to ask him tonight if he wants to attend your wedding with me. Please wish me luck, I moaned.

You haven't questioned him yet, I see. She exploded.

"No." I chuckled "We don't often go out in public as a pair. We share a bed."

So ask him and let me know, please! She pushed me outside.

I chuckled as I put my boots on. Sara was both my sister and my dearest friend. I told her the whole truth. In addition to my one-night stand with Adam.

I kept quiet to her about the fact that I may wish to date kelvin. a trustworthy connection.

When I arrived at the house, Kelvin was eating pizza at the dinner table. He turned to face me as I got some pizza and sat down across from him.

How is Saras doing? He queried.

I need to speak with you about something, um. I declared.

"I'm not accompanying you to your sister's wedding." Before I could even inquire, he lost his cool.

Why not, I questioned.

"Since you're not my wife or girlfriend." He barked.

"You still have time to go," I muttered.

"Or you might not be a girl like that." He said, "What took place to you? You were so awesome back then."

"Kelvin, I'm a lady." I lost it.

I'm a guy, too. He replied sharply.

"I want to get married and have a family someday," I said.

Oh, yes. Because it appears to me that all you want is to have sex, he said with a grin.

Word slur.

"Kelvin, I want to be your girlfriend!" As tears streamed down my cheeks, I shouted and immediately wiped them away.

Who are you? He exploded.

You're like my best buddy, I guess. And when I was out on my date with Adam, all I could think about was how lovely it would be if it were you, I said.

You are aware that I am not a relationship man. He barked.

I am aware of kelvin. I exhaled, "I believe you need to go."

You want me to go? he questioned.

"Yes." I answered, "After all the time we've spent together, if all you want from me is sex, then sure. You should go, please."

"I don't. My dearest buddy, you." He sighed.

But because you continue to date other women, you don't want me to be your girlfriend. He shrugged, "Please leave," and I gasped.

Kelvin departed fast but left all of his belongings behind, which indicated to me that he intended to return eventually.

I hurriedly reached for my phone and phoned the number.

"Hello?" A groggy voice questioned.

Adam, can you come over?

Chapter 10

Ten days till the wedding.

Adam and Kelvin have both been missing for eleven days.

Every day with Adam gets better and better. He's funny and kind. Although he has all of kelvin's traits, he is not kelvin.

"Are you thinking about him?" Sara asked me when I was sitting at the bridal shop.

Yes, I said as I changed into my maid of honor attire.

What kind is it? She laughed.

"kelvin." I moaned "I like Adam. He meets every need I had for a partner."

But she persisted.

He is not Kelvin, however. I muttered: "I don't make pizza with him at three in the morning. I don't complain to him for hours on end. He's just not kelvin."

It seems like your choice was driven by your emotions. She grinned at me.

That's very corny. I took a shot, grinned, and moved away from the counter. "Okay! Dinner before the next practice. For me, there will be a date."

Which will you be bringing? She beamed.

"None. I'll figure something out, however." I said, "See you later," as I put on my sweater.

I spotted Kelvin's vehicle in the driveway when I got home. I resisted going to see him. I wasn't ready for our meeting.

I moaned as I walked in and saw Kelvin waiting for me.

"Please exit the room, kelvin. I prefer not to" As I began to explain, he turned to face me.

and she was holding a toddler.

My daughter Brea is here. He smiled.

? her father What? He brought his daughter to me. How should I make my point?

Hello, sweetie. I smiled as she laughed at me.

"I have a family already." He said, "I have one already and I'm not sure whether I want more kids."

I cried out, "kelvin-"

I'm unsure about my desires. But I know that in some way, I need you in my life, he said.

Sweet.

nice

No, really. But the fact that Kelvin moved was what mattered to me.

I take it that you came here to inform me that you are unsure of your intentions toward me. I smiled.

"Uh...yeah." He grinned in response.

"Okay."

Chapter 11

5 days before the wedding.

Where is Brea now? As Kelvin sat down on the sofa, I questioned.

With her mother. He shrugged.

What's wrong, I enquired.

"I need to share something with you." He swallowed.

I inquired, "Tell me something."

He swallowed, "Yeah."

Okay, I questioned.

I had a bed with Brea's mother. He declared.

My gut became sick to my chest.

You what, He stood up as I shouted.

It happened by mistake. I retreated as he reached out to touch me.

"You never have sex! before me. Why her then? Why do you suddenly feel the need to have sex with everyone? I screamed.

I don't have sex with everyone, He declared.

I've finished.

"I thought you cared about me," I shouted. You claimed to have.

I do," he complained.

"You don't, no. You wouldn't have slept with someone else if you did! I screamed.

"You had a bed with Adam!" He screamed.

That was before we decided to be together. "I haven't done anything since then," I screamed back. Adam at work and everywhere else has been disregarded FOR YOU!

"I apologize." He said "sorry,"

I grabbed my sweatshirt and slammed the door behind me as I left him in the home. I kept driving till I ran out of places to go.

My face was dripping with tears when I knocked on the door. My sister scowled at me as she opened the door.

I complained, "He slept with someone else."

Chapter 12

THE WEDDING DAY

"Come on, just let me adjust your tie and we are set to go." I grinned, "Hey I appreciate you coming with me as a buddy."

"Of course." Adam grinned.

"How are you feeling?" He questioned.

"Fine. I vomited this morning." I shrugged.

"Did you inform kelvin yet?" He asked.

"No." I shrugged, "I don't know what to say to him."

"Sooner or later you'll have to inform him." He said.

"I know." I gulped as I straightened his tie and we headed into the ceremony.

The Wedding was gorgeous and I gave my speech just as I practiced it. It was the ideal day for my sister.

I changed into some decent clothing for the reception and walked directly into a man with dark hair and eyes who gazed down at me like I was a piece of trash.

"Watch where you're walking." He snapped at me.

"Excuse you." I snapped back.

"Sorry I umm..." He swept his eyes down my body and sneered, "I'm Kaleb."

"Jovita." I smiled as I felt my cheeks turn pink.

"Do you want to uhm, buy some food?" He asked.

"Of course," I said.

We bought some plates and sat down as everyone around us spoke.

"Excuse me." A strong voice flooded my ears as I turned to see kelvin.

"kelvin!" I gasped as I rose and shoved him into the next room, "What are you doing here?"

"I come to tell you something." He breathed out.

"No, I have to tell you something."

"No, let me." He exclaimed.

"I'm pregnant." I blurted out.

"Is it mine?" He inquired.

"They." I corrected it.

"They?" He questioned.

"Twins," I said.

"Are THEY mine?"

He asked.

"I don't know."

Chapter 13

kelvin, "Ahh." He pushed himself inside of me, and I groaned.

He grasped my ass as I was riding him, and I gasped for oxygen. He tensed up as I pushed down even more forcefully than before, allowing myself to fall directly upon him.

"Bitch, you love this dick, don't you?" You've learnt some new movements, I whimpered in response as he moaned.

"Be quiet." As I let go, both he and I moaned.

As I sat on him and attempted to regain my breath, he moaned. As I got off and put my clothes on, I gasped for oxygen.

I had to go. I chuckled and said, "I need to make an arrangement with Kaleb since I'm going to rehab in a few months."

"Why you persist in hanging around with that moron is beyond me. My twins were just born last year, you." He sighed.

"Kaleb is adored by the twins." And he's kind to me, I added.

Doesn't fisk you as much as I do, however. He grinned.

"I know." I said, "Kaleb has my goodbye. I made my decision a few weeks ago. I'm not interested in him, therefore."

Oh yeah? he questioned.

"Yeah." I sighed "I need to pick up the twins from childcare. Come along? And please tell Kaleb to me."

"Okay."

After picking up Bird and Zander from daycare, we went directly home, where Kaleb was waiting for me at the table.

Kelvin entered the building after I did. The moment I put the twins down, Kaleb stared at Kelvin as the children fled.

Why is he in this place? Kaleb enquired.

"Kaleb, I must go. "For kelvin," I said.

"What?!" I was smacked across the face with his uplifted palm, which caused me to fall to the ground.

He was pressed against the wall when Kelvin grabbed him by the shirt. As I positioned myself between them and raised my arms to Kelvin's face, I yelled.

I said, "Stop!"

Grab the twins, Jovita. Kelvin replied as I picked up the two infants and headed out.

With the exception of the twins' belongings, I left everything of my stuff behind with Kaleb.

Kelvin climbed up into bed with me after putting the twins to sleep. I sat down and made an effort not to cry.

"I understand that you are an addict because you were raped." He said, "And I know you built this wall and didn't allow anybody in."

I feigned interruption, "kelvin-"

"I also understand that you tend to remain quiet when you're unhappy. Jovita, you are my favorite. As you attend rehab, I'll watch the twins. We'll be here waiting for you when you come back as well."

I turned over on my side and grinned at kelvin, who grinned back and said, "I love you too, kelvin."

www.ingramcontent.com/pod-product-compliance
Lightning Source LLC
LaVergne TN
LVHW050327160826
845677LV00014B/3561